**Praise for Jeffrey Archer's novels**

'If there was a Nobel prize for storytelling,
Archer would win'
*Daily Telegraph*

'Probably the greatest storyteller of our age'
*Mail on Sunday*

'The man's a genius . . . the strength and
excitement of the idea carries all before it'
*Evening Standard*

'A storyteller in the class of Alexandre Dumas'
*Washington Post*

'Archer has a gift for storytelling that can
only be described as genius'
*Daily Telegraph*

'Back in top form . . . Archer's imagination at its most
sublime . . . an entertaining, pacey page-turner'
*Sunday Times*

'Few are more famous than Archer for keeping
the pages turning . . . an extravagant romp –
possibly his best'
*The Times*

# Four Warned

JEFFREY ARCHER, whose novels and short stories include *Kane and Abel*, *A Prisoner of Birth* and *Cat O' Nine Tales*, has topped the bestseller lists around the world, with sales of over 270 million copies.

He is the only author ever to have been a number one bestseller in fiction (fifteen times), short stories (three times) and non-fiction (*The Prison Diaries*).

The author is married with two sons and lives in London and Cambridge.

www.jeffreyarcher.com
Facebook.com/JeffreyArcherAuthor
@Jeffrey_Archer

Also by JEFFREY ARCHER

NOVELS
Not a Penny More, Not a Penny Less
Shall We Tell the President?
Kane and Abel    The Prodigal Daughter
First Among Equals    A Matter of Honour
As the Crow Flies    Honour Among Thieves
The Fourth Estate    The Eleventh Commandment
Sons of Fortune    False Impression
The Gospel According to Judas
(*with the assistance of Professor Francis J. Moloney*)
A Prisoner of Birth    Paths of Glory
Only Time Will Tell    The Sins of the Father
Best Kept Secret

SHORT STORIES
A Quiver Full of Arrows    A Twist in the Tale
Twelve Red Herrings    The Collected Short Stories
To Cut a Long Story Short    Cat O' Nine Tales
And Thereby Hangs a Tale

PLAYS
Beyond Reasonable Doubt    Exclusive    The Accused

PRISON DIARIES
Volume One – Belmarsh: Hell
Volume Two – Wayland: Purgatory
Volume Three – North Sea Camp: Heaven

SCREENPLAYS
Mallory: Walking Off the Map    False Impression

# JEFFREY ARCHER

## FOUR WARNED

PAN BOOKS

'Never Stop on the Motorway'
first published 1994 in *Twelve Red Herrings* by HarperCollins Publishers
First published by Pan Books 2004

'The Queen's Birthday Telegram'
first published 2010 by Macmillan in *And Thereby Hangs a Tale*
First published by Pan Books 2010

'Stuck on You' first published 2010 by Macmillan in *And Thereby Hangs a Tale*
First published by Pan Books 2010

'Don't Drink the Water' first published 2007 in *Cat O' Nine Tales* by Macmillan
First published by Pan Books 2007

This edition published 2014 by Pan Books
an imprint of Pan Macmillan, a division of Macmillan Publishers Limited
Pan Macmillan, 20 New Wharf Road, London N1 9RR
Basingstoke and Oxford
Associated companies throughout the world
www.panmacmillan.com

ISBN 978-1-4472-5248-1

1 3 5 7 9 8 6 4 2

A CIP catalogue record for this book is available from the British Library.

Typeset by Birdy Book Design
Printed and bound by CPI Group (UK) Ltd, Croydon, CR0 4YY

Visit **www.panmacmillan.com** to read more about all our books
and to buy them. You will also find features, author interviews and
news of any author events, and you can sign up for e-newsletters so
that you're always first to hear about our new releases.

# Contents

* Based on true incidents

# Never Stop on the Motorway

## (from *Twelve Red Herrings*)

Diana had been hoping to get away by five o'clock, so she could be at the farm in time for dinner. She tried not to show her true feelings when at 4.37 p.m. her deputy, Phil Haskins, gave her a complex twelve-page document that needed her sign-off before it could be sent out to the client. Haskins reminded her that they had lost two similar contracts that week.

It was always the same on a Friday. The phones would go quiet in the middle of the afternoon. Then, just as she thought she could slip away, some paperwork would land on her desk. One glance at this document and Diana knew there would be no chance of leaving before six.

The demands of being a single parent as well as a director of a small but thriving City firm meant there were few moments left in any day to relax. So when it came to the one weekend in four that her children James and Caroline spent with her ex-husband, Diana would try to leave the office a little earlier than usual to avoid getting caught up in the weekend traffic.

She read through the first page of the contract slowly and made a couple of changes, aware that any mistake made in haste on a Friday night could be regretted in the weeks to come. She glanced at the clock on her desk as she signed the final page of the document. It was just flicking over to 5.51 p.m.

Diana gathered up her bag and walked purposefully towards the door, dropping the document on Phil's desk without bothering to wish him a good weekend. She suspected that the paperwork had been on his desk since nine o'clock that morning, but that holding onto it until late afternoon was his only means of revenge now that she had been made head of department. Once she was safely in the lift, she pressed the button for the basement car park, working out that the delay would probably add an extra hour to her journey.

She stepped out of the lift, walked over to her Audi estate car, unlocked the door and threw her bag onto the back seat. When she drove up onto the street, the stream of twilight traffic was just about keeping pace with the pinstriped people on the pavements who, like worker ants, were hurrying towards the nearest hole in the ground.

She flicked on the radio for the six o'clock news. The chimes of Big Ben rang out, before spokesmen from each of the three main political parties gave their views on the European election results. John Major was refusing to comment on his future. The Conservative Party's explanation for its poor showing was that only thirty-six per cent of the country had bothered to go to the polls. Diana felt guilty – she was among the sixty-four per cent who had failed to vote.

The newscaster moved on to say that the situation in Bosnia was still desperate, and that the UN was threatening dire action if the Serbs – and their leader, Radovan Karadzik – didn't come to an agreement with the other warring parties. Diana's mind began to drift – such a threat was hardly news any longer. She thought that if she turned on the radio in a year's time they would probably be repeating the story word for word.

As her car crawled round Russell Square, she began to think about the weekend ahead. It had been over a year since John had told her that he had met another woman and wanted a divorce. She still wondered why, after seven years of marriage, she hadn't been more shocked – or at least angry – at his betrayal. Since her appointment as a company director, she had to admit they had spent less and less time together. And perhaps she had become numbed by the fact that a third of the married couples in Britain were now divorced or separated. Her parents had been unable to hide their disappointment, but then they had been married for forty-two years.

The divorce had been friendly enough, as John, who earned less than she did – one of their problems, perhaps – had given in to most of her demands. She had kept the flat in south west London, the Audi estate and the children, to whom John was allowed access one weekend in four. He would have picked them up from school earlier that afternoon, and, as usual, he would return them to the flat in Putney around seven on Sunday evening.

Diana would go to almost any lengths to avoid being left on her own in the flat when they weren't around. Although she regularly grumbled about being landed with the job of bringing up two children without a father, she missed them greatly the moment they were out of sight.

She hadn't taken a lover and she didn't sleep around. None of the senior staff at the office had ever gone further than asking her out to lunch. Perhaps because only three of them were unmarried – and not without reason. The one person she might have considered having a relationship with had made it very clear that he only wanted to spend the *night* with her, not the days.

In any case, Diana had decided long ago that if she was to be taken seriously as the company's first female director, an office affair – however casual or short-lived – could only end in tears. Men are so vain, she thought. A woman only had to make one mistake and she was immediately labelled as loose. Then every other man in the office either smirks behind your back, or treats your thigh like the arm of his chair.

Diana groaned as she came to a halt at yet another red light. In twenty minutes she had only covered a couple of miles. She opened the glove box on the passenger side and fumbled in the dark for a cassette. She found one and pressed it into the slot, hoping it would be Pavarotti. Instead, she was greeted by the forceful tones of Gloria Gaynor assuring her 'I will survive'. She smiled and thought about her friend Daniel, as the light changed to green.

She and Daniel had read Economics together at Bristol University in the early 1980s. They had been friends but never lovers. Then Daniel met Rachael, who was a year below them, and from that moment he had never looked at another woman. They married the day he graduated, and after they returned from their honeymoon Daniel took over the management of his father's farm in Bedfordshire.

Three children had followed soon after each other, and Diana had been proud when she was asked to be godmother to Sophie, the eldest. Daniel and Rachael had now been married for twelve years, and Diana felt confident that they wouldn't be disappointing *their* parents with any suggestion of a divorce. Although they thought she led an exciting and fulfilling life in the City, Diana often envied their gentle and uncomplicated lives.

She was often asked to spend the weekend with them in the country. But for every two or three invitations Daniel gave, she only accepted one – not because she wouldn't have liked to join them more, but because since her divorce she had no desire to take advantage of their kindness.

Although she enjoyed her work, it had been a bloody week. Two contracts had fallen through, her son James had been dropped from the school football team, and Caroline had never stopped telling her that her *father* didn't mind her watching television when she ought to be doing her homework.

Another traffic light changed to red.

It took Diana nearly an hour to travel the seven miles out of the city, and when she reached the first dual carriageway, she glanced up at the A1 sign. It was more out of habit than to seek guidance, because she knew every yard of the road from her office to the farm. She tried to increase her speed, but it was quite impossible, as both lanes stayed stubbornly crowded.

'Damn.' She had forgotten to get them a present, even a decent bottle of claret. 'Damn,' she said again. Daniel and Rachael always did the giving. She began to wonder if she could pick something up on the way, then remembered there was nothing but service stations between here and the farm. She couldn't turn up with yet another box of chocolates they'd never eat. When she reached the roundabout that led onto the A1, she managed to push the car over fifty for the first time. She began to relax, letting her mind drift with the music.

There was no warning. Although she quickly slammed her foot on the brakes, it was already too late. There was a dull thump from the front bumper, and a slight shudder rocked the car.

A small black creature had shot across her path, and despite her quick reactions, she hadn't been able to avoid hitting it. Diana swung onto the hard shoulder and screeched to a halt, wondering if the animal could still be alive. She reversed slowly back to the spot where she thought she had hit it as the traffic roared past her.

And then she saw it, lying on the grass verge – a cat that had crossed the road for the tenth time. She stepped out of the car, and walked towards the lifeless body. Suddenly Diana felt sick. She had two cats of her own, and she knew she would never be able to tell the children what she had done. She picked up the dead animal and laid it gently in the ditch by the side of the road.

'I'm so sorry,' she said, feeling a little silly. She gave it one last look before walking back to her car. Ironically, she had chosen the Audi for its safety features.

She climbed back into the car and switched on the ignition to find Gloria Gaynor was still belting out her opinion of men. She turned her off, and tried to stop thinking about the cat as she waited for a gap in the traffic large enough to allow her to ease her way back into the slow lane. She eventually succeeded, but was still unable to erase the dead cat from her mind.

Diana had sped up to fifty again when she suddenly became aware of a pair of headlights shining through her rear windscreen. She put up her arm and waved in her rear-view mirror, but the lights continued to dazzle her. She slowed down to allow the vehicle to pass, but the driver showed no sign of doing so. Diana began to wonder if there was something wrong with her car. Was one of her lights not working? Was the exhaust smoking? Was . . .

She decided to speed up and put some distance between herself and the vehicle behind, but it stayed within a few yards of her bumper. She tried to snatch a look at the driver in her rear-view mirror, but it was hard to see much in the harshness of the lights. As her eyes became more used to the glare, she could just see the outline of a large black van bearing down on her, and what looked like a young man behind the wheel. He seemed to be waving at her.

Diana slowed down again as she approached the next roundabout, giving him every chance to overtake her on the outside lane, but once again he didn't take the opportunity. He just sat on her bumper, his headlights still bright. She waited for a small gap in the traffic coming from her right. When one appeared she slammed her foot on the accelerator, shot across the roundabout and sped on up the A1.

She was rid of him at last. She was just beginning to relax and to think about her god-daughter Sophie, who always waited up so that Diana could read to her, when suddenly those high-beam headlights were glaring through her rear windscreen and blinding her again. If anything, they were even closer to her than before.

She slowed down, he slowed down. She accelerated, he accelerated. She tried to think what she could do next, and began waving frantically at passing motorists as they sped by, but they were unaware of her situation. Diana tried to think of other ways she might alert someone. She suddenly recalled that when she had joined the board of the company, they had suggested she have a car phone fitted. Diana had decided it could wait until the car went in for its next service, which should have been a fortnight ago.

She brushed her hand across her forehead and wiped away a film of perspiration. She thought for a moment, then moved her car into the fast lane. The van swung across after her, and hovered so close to her bumper that she became fearful that if she so much as touched her brakes she might unwittingly cause a huge pile-up.

Diana took the car up to ninety, but the van wouldn't be shaken off. She pushed her foot further down on the accelerator and touched a hundred, but it still remained less than a car's length behind.

She flicked her headlights onto high-beam, turned on her hazard lights and blasted her horn at anyone who dared to remain in her path. She could only hope that the police might see her, wave her onto the hard shoulder and book her for speeding. A fine would be infinitely better than a crash with a young tearaway, she thought, as the Audi estate passed a hundred and ten for the first time in its life. But the black van couldn't be shaken off.

Without warning, she swerved back into the middle lane and took her foot off the gas, causing the van to draw level with her, which gave her a chance to look at the driver for the first time. He was wearing a black leather jacket and pointing menacingly at her. She shook her fist at him and accelerated away, but he simply swung across behind her like an Olympic runner determined not to allow his rival to break clear.

And then she remembered something, and felt sick for a second time that night. 'Oh my God,' she shouted aloud in terror. In a flood, the details of the murder that had taken place on the same road a few months before came rushing back to her. A woman had been raped before having her throat cut with a knife with a serrated edge and dumped in a ditch.

For weeks there had been signs posted on the A1 appealing to passing motorists to phone a certain number if they had any information that might assist the police with their inquiries. The signs had now gone, but the police were still searching for the killer. Diana began to tremble as she remembered their warning to all woman drivers: 'Never stop on the motorway'.

A few seconds later she saw a road sign she knew well. She had reached it far sooner than she had anticipated. In three miles she would have to leave the motorway for the slip road that led to the farm. She began to pray that if she took her usual turning, the black-jacketed man would continue on up the A1 and she would finally be rid of him.

Diana decided that the time had come for her

to speed him on his way. She swung back into the fast lane and once again put her foot down on the accelerator. She reached a hundred miles per hour for the second time as she sped past the two-mile sign. Her body was now covered in sweat, and the speedometer touched a hundred and ten. She checked her rear-view mirror, but he was still right behind her. She would have to pick the exact moment if she was to execute her plan successfully.

With a mile to go, she began to look to her left, to make sure her timing would be perfect. She no longer needed to check in her mirror. She knew that he would still be there.

The next signpost showed three diagonal white lines, warning her that she ought to be on the inside lane if she meant to leave the motorway at the next junction. She kept the car in the outside lane at a hundred miles per hour until she spotted a large enough gap. Two white lines appeared by the roadside. Diana knew she would have only one chance to make her escape.

As she passed the sign with a single white line on it she suddenly swung across the road at ninety miles per hour, causing cars in the middle and inside lanes to throw on their brakes and blast out their angry opinions. But Diana didn't care what they thought of her, because she was now travelling down the slip road to safety, and the black van was speeding on up the A1.

She laughed out loud with relief. To her right, she could see the steady flow of traffic on the motorway. But then her laugh turned to a scream as she saw the black van cut sharply across the motorway in front of a lorry, mount the grass verge and career onto the slip road, swinging from side to side. It nearly drove over the edge and into a ditch, but somehow managed to steady itself, ending up a few yards behind her, its lights once again glaring through her rear windscreen.

When she reached the top of the slip road, Diana turned left in the direction of the farm, frantically trying to work out what she should do next. The nearest town was about twelve miles away on the main road, and the farm was only seven, but five of those miles were down a winding, unlit country lane. She checked her petrol meter. It was nearing empty, but there should still be enough in the tank for her to consider either option. There was less than a mile to go before she reached the turning, so she had only a minute in which to make up her mind.

With a hundred yards to go, she settled on

the farm. Despite the unlit lane, she knew every twist and turn, and she felt confident that her pursuer wouldn't. Once she reached the farm she could be out of the car and inside the house long before he could catch her. In any case, once he saw the farmhouse, surely he would flee?

The minute was up. Diana touched the brakes and skidded into a country road lit only by the moon.

Diana banged the palms of her hands on the steering wheel. Had she made the wrong decision? She glanced up at her rear-view mirror. Had he given up? Of course he hadn't. The back of a Land Rover loomed up in front of her. Diana slowed down, waiting for a corner she knew well, where the road widened slightly. She held her breath, crashed into third gear, and overtook. Would a head-on collision be preferable to a cut throat?

She rounded the bend and saw an empty road ahead of her. Once again she pressed her foot down, this time managing to put a clear seventy, perhaps even a hundred, yards between her and her pursuer, but this only offered her a few moments' relief. Before long the familiar headlights came bearing down on her once again.

With each bend Diana was able to gain a

little time as the van continued to lurch from side to side, unfamiliar with the road. But she never managed a clear break of more than a few seconds. She checked the mileometer. From the turn-off on the main road to the farm it was just over five miles, and she must have covered about two by now. She began to watch each tenth of a mile clicking up, terrified at the thought of the van overtaking her and forcing her into the ditch. She stuck firmly to the centre of the road.

Another mile passed, and still he clung on to her. Suddenly she saw a car coming towards her. She switched her headlights to full beam and pressed on the horn. The other car retaliated by copying her actions, which caused her to slow down and brush against the hedgerow as they shot past each other. She checked the mileometer once again. Only two miles to go.

Diana would slow down and then speed up at each familiar bend in the road, making sure the van was never given enough room to pull level with her. She tried to concentrate on what she should do once the farmhouse came into sight. She reckoned that the drive leading up to the house must be about half a mile long. It was full of potholes and bumps which Daniel had often explained he couldn't afford to have repaired. But at least it was only wide enough for one car.

The gate to the driveway was usually left open for her, though on the rare occasion Daniel had forgotten, and she'd had to get out of the car and open it for herself. She couldn't risk that tonight. If the gate was closed, she would have to travel on to the next town and stop outside the Crimson Kipper, which was always crowded at this time on a Friday night, or, if she could find it, on the steps of the local police station. She checked her petrol gauge again. It was now touching red. 'Oh my God,' she said, realising she might not have enough petrol to reach the town.

She could only pray that Daniel had remembered to leave the gate open.

She swerved out of the next bend and sped up, but once again she managed to gain only a few yards, and she knew that within seconds he would be back in place. He was. For the next few hundred yards they remained within feet of each other, and she felt certain he would run into the back of her. She didn't once dare to touch her brakes – if they crashed in that lane, far from any help, she would have no hope of getting away from him.

She checked her mileometer. A mile to go.

'The gate must be open. It *must* be open,' she prayed. As she swung round the next bend, she could make out the outline of the farmhouse in the distance. She almost screamed with relief when she saw that the lights were on in the downstairs rooms.

She shouted, 'Thank God!' then remembered the gate again, and changed her plea to 'Dear God, let it be open.' She would know what needed to be done as soon as she came round the last bend. 'Let it be open, just this once,' she pleaded. 'I'll never ask for anything again, ever.' She swung round the final bend only inches ahead of the black van. 'Please, please, please.' And then she saw the gate.

It was open.

Her clothes were now drenched in sweat. She slowed down, wrenched the gearbox into second, and threw the car between the gap and into the bumpy driveway, hitting the gatepost on her right-hand side as she careered on up towards the house. The van didn't hesitate to follow her, and was still only inches behind as she straightened up. Diana kept her hand pressed down on the horn as the car bounced and lurched over the mounds and potholes.

Flocks of startled crows flapped out of overhead branches, screeching as they shot into the air. Diana began screaming, 'Daniel! Daniel!' Two hundred yards ahead of her, the porch light went on.

Her headlights were now shining onto the front of the house, and her hand was still pressed on the horn. With a hundred yards to go, she spotted Daniel coming out of the front door, but she didn't slow down, and neither did the van behind her. With fifty yards to go she began flashing her lights at Daniel. She could now make out the puzzled, anxious look on his face.

With thirty yards to go she threw on her brakes. The heavy estate car skidded across the gravel in front of the house, coming to a halt in the flower bed just below the kitchen window. She heard the screech of brakes behind her. The leather-jacketed man, unfamiliar with the terrain, had been unable to react quickly enough, and as soon as his wheels touched the gravelled area he began to skid out of control. A second later the van came crashing into the back of her car, slamming it against the wall of the house and shattering the glass in the kitchen window.

Diana leapt out of the car, screaming, 'Daniel!

Get a gun, get a gun!' She pointed back at the van. 'That bastard's been chasing me for the last twenty miles!'

The man jumped out of the van and began limping towards them. Diana ran into the house. Daniel followed and grabbed a shotgun, normally reserved for rabbits, that was leaning against the wall. He ran back outside to face the unwelcome visitor, who had come to a halt by the back of Diana's Audi.

Daniel raised the shotgun to his shoulder and stared straight at him. 'Don't move or I'll shoot,' he said calmly. And then he remembered the gun wasn't loaded. Diana ducked back out of the house, but remained several yards behind him.

'Not me! Not me!' shouted the leather-jacketed youth, as Rachael appeared in the doorway.

'What's going on?' she asked nervously.

'Ring for the police,' was all Daniel said, and his wife quickly disappeared back into the house.

Daniel advanced towards the terrified-looking young man, the gun aimed squarely at his chest.

'Not me! Not me!' he shouted again, pointing at the Audi. 'He's in the car!' He quickly turned to face Diana. 'I saw him get in when you were parked on the hard shoulder. What else could I have done? You just wouldn't pull over.'

Daniel advanced cautiously towards the rear door of the car and ordered the young man to open it slowly, while he kept the gun aimed at his chest.

The youth opened the door, and quickly took a pace backwards. The three of them stared down at a man crouched on the floor of the car. In his right hand he held a long-bladed knife with a serrated edge. Daniel swung the barrel of the gun down to point at him, but said nothing.

The sound of a police siren could just be heard in the distance.

# The Queen's Birthday Telegram

## (from *And Thereby Hangs a Tale*)

*Her Majesty the Queen sends her congratulations
to Albert Webber on the occasion of his 100th
birthday, and wishes him many more years of
good health and happiness.*

Albert was still smiling after he had read the
message for the twentieth time.

'You will be next, ducks,' he said as he passed
the royal message across to his wife. Betty only
had to read the telegram once for a broad smile
to appear on her face too.

The festivities had begun a week earlier,
building up to a celebration party at the town
hall. Albert's photograph had appeared on the
front page of the *Somerset Gazette* that morning, and he had been interviewed on *BBC Points
West*, his wife seated proudly by his side.

His Worship the Mayor of Street, Councillor Ted Harding, and the leader of the local council, Councillor Brocklebank, were waiting on the town hall steps to greet the honoured guest.

Albert was escorted to the mayor's parlour where he was introduced to Mr David Heathcote-Amory, the local Member of Parliament, as well as the local MEP, although when asked later he couldn't remember her name.

After several more photographs had been taken, Albert was ushered through to a large reception room where over a hundred invited guests were waiting to greet him. As he entered the room he was welcomed by a spontaneous burst of applause, and people he'd never met before began shaking hands with him.

At 3.27 p.m., the precise minute Albert had been born in 1907, the old man, surrounded by his five children, eleven grandchildren and nineteen great-grandchildren, thrust a silver-handled knife into a three-tier cake. This simple act was greeted by another burst of applause, followed by cries of *speech, speech, speech!*

Albert had prepared a few words, but as quiet fell in the room, they went straight out of his head.

'Say something,' said Betty, giving her husband a gentle nudge in the ribs.

He blinked, looked around at the expectant crowd, paused and said, 'Thank you very much.'

Once the people realised that was all he was going to say, someone began to sing 'Happy Birthday', and within moments everyone was joining in. Albert managed to blow out seven of the hundred candles before the younger members of the family came to his rescue, which was greeted by even more laughter and clapping.

Once the applause had died down, the mayor rose to his feet, tugged at the lapels of his black and gold braided gown and cleared his throat, before delivering a far longer speech.

'My fellow citizens,' he began, 'we are gathered together today to celebrate the birthday, the one hundredth birthday, of Albert Webber, a much-loved member of our community. Albert was born in Street on the fifteenth of April 1907. He married his wife Betty at Holy Trinity Church in 1931, and spent his working life at C. and J. Clark's, our local shoe factory.

'In fact,' he continued, 'Albert has spent his entire life in Street, with the notable exception of four years when he served as a private soldier in the Somerset Light Infantry. When the war ended in 1945, Albert was discharged from the army and returned to Street to take up his old job as a leather cutter at Clark's. At the age of sixty, he retired as Deputy Floor Manager. But you can't get rid of Albert that easily, because he then took on part-time work as a night watchman, a responsibility he carried out until his seventieth birthday.'

The mayor waited for the laughter to fade before he continued. 'From his early days, Albert has always been a loyal supporter of Street Football Club, rarely missing a Cobblers' home game, and indeed the club has recently made him an honorary life member. Albert also played darts for the Crown and Anchor, and was a member of that team when they were runners-up in the town's pub championship.

'I'm sure you will all agree,' concluded the mayor, 'that Albert has led a colourful and interesting life, which we all hope will continue for many years to come, not least because in three years' time we will be celebrating the same landmark for his dear wife Betty. It's hard to believe, looking at her,' said the mayor, turning towards Mrs Webber, 'that in 2010 she will also be one hundred.'

'Hear, hear,' said several voices, and Betty shyly bowed her head as Albert leaned across and took her hand.

After several other important people had said

a few words, and many more had had their photographs taken with Albert, the mayor walked with his two guests out of the town hall to a waiting Rolls-Royce, and told the chauffeur to drive Mr and Mrs Webber home.

Albert and Betty sat in the back of the car holding hands. Neither of them had ever been in a Rolls-Royce before, and certainly not in one driven by a chauffeur.

By the time the car drew up outside their council house in Marne Terrace, they were both so exhausted and so full of salmon sandwiches and birthday cake that it wasn't long before they went to bed. The last thing Albert murmured before turning out his bedside light was, 'Well, it will be your turn next, ducks, and I'm determined to live another three years so we can celebrate your hundredth together.'

'I don't want all that fuss made over me when my time comes,' she said. But Albert had already fallen asleep.

*   *   *

Not a lot happened in Albert and Betty Webber's life during the next three years: a few minor ailments, but nothing life threatening, and the birth of their first great-great-grandchild, Jude.

When the historic day approached for the second Webber to celebrate a hundredth birthday, Albert had become so frail that Betty insisted the party be held at their home and only include the family. Albert reluctantly agreed, and didn't tell his wife how much he'd been looking forward to returning to the town hall and once again being driven home in the mayor's Rolls-Royce.

The new mayor was equally disappointed, as he'd hoped that the occasion would guarantee his photograph on the front page of the local paper.

When the great day dawned, Betty received over a hundred cards, letters and messages from well-wishers, but to Albert's profound dismay, there was no telegram from the Queen. He assumed the Post Office was to blame and that it would surely be delivered the following day. It wasn't.

'Don't fuss, Albert,' Betty insisted. 'Her Majesty is a very busy lady and she must have far more important things on her mind.'

But Albert did fuss. When no telegram arrived the next day, or the following week, he felt a pang of disappointment for his wife who seemed to be taking the whole affair in such good spirits. However, after another week, and still no sign of a telegram, Albert decided the time had come to take the matter into his own hands.

Every Thursday morning, Eileen, their youngest daughter, aged seventy-three, would come to pick up Betty and drive her into town to go shopping. In reality this usually turned out to be just window shopping, as Betty couldn't believe the prices the shops had the nerve to charge. She could remember when a loaf of bread cost a penny, and a pound a week was a working wage.

That Thursday, Albert waited for them to leave the house, then he stood by the window until the car had disappeared around the corner. Once they were out of sight, he shuffled off to his little den, where he sat by the phone, going over the exact words he would say if he was put through.

After a little while, and once he felt he was word perfect, he looked up at the framed telegram on the wall above him. It gave him enough confidence to pick up the phone and dial a six-digit number.

'Directory Enquiries. What number do you require?'

'Buckingham Palace,' said Albert, hoping his voice sounded full of authority.

There was a slight pause, but the operator finally said, 'One moment please.'

Albert waited patiently, although he quite expected to be told that the number was either unlisted or ex-directory. A moment later the operator was back on the line and read out the number.

'Can you please repeat that?' asked a surprised Albert as he took the top off his biro. 'Zero two zero, seven seven six six, seven three zero zero. 'Thank you,' he said, before putting the phone down. Several minutes passed before he gathered enough courage to pick it back up again.

Albert dialled the number with a shaky hand. He listened to the familiar ringing tone and was just about to put the phone back down when a woman's voice said, 'Buckingham Palace, how may I help you?'

'I'd like to speak to someone about a one hundredth birthday,' said Albert, repeating the exact words he had memorised.

'Who shall I say is calling?'

'Mr Albert Webber.'

'Hold the line please, Mr Webber.'

This was Albert's last chance of escape, but before he could put the phone down, another voice came on the line.

'Humphrey Cranshaw speaking.'

The last time Albert had heard a voice like that was when he was serving in the army. 'Good morning, sir,' he said nervously. 'I was hoping you might be able to help me.'

'I certainly will if I can, Mr Webber,' replied the courtier.

'Three years ago I celebrated my hundredth birthday,' said Albert, returning to his well-rehearsed script.

'Many congratulations,' said Cranshaw.

'Thank you, sir,' said Albert, 'but that isn't the reason why I'm calling. You see, on that occasion Her Majesty the Queen was kind enough to send me a telegram, which is now framed on the wall in front of me, and which I will treasure for the rest of my life.'

'How kind of you to say so, Mr Webber.'

'But I wondered,' said Albert, gaining in confidence, 'if Her Majesty still sends telegrams when people reach their hundredth birthday?'

'She most certainly does,' replied Cranshaw. 'I know that it gives Her Majesty great pleasure to continue the tradition, even though so many more people now reach that magnificent milestone.'

'Oh, that is most gratifying to hear, Mr Cranshaw,' said Albert, 'because my dear wife celebrated her hundredth birthday some two weeks ago, but sadly has not yet received a telegram from the Queen.'

'I am sorry to hear that, Mr Webber,' said the courtier. 'It must be an administrative oversight on our part. Please allow me to check. What is your wife's full name?'

'Elizabeth Violet Webber, née Braithwaite,' said Albert with pride.

'Just give me a moment, Mr Webber,' said Cranshaw, 'while I check our records.'

This time Albert had to wait a little longer before Mr Cranshaw came back on the line. 'I am sorry to have kept you waiting, Mr Webber, but you'll be pleased to learn that we have traced your wife's telegram.'

'Oh, I'm so glad,' said Albert. 'May I ask when she can expect to receive it?'

There was a moment's hesitation before the courtier said, 'Her Majesty sent a telegram to your wife to congratulate her on reaching her hundredth birthday some five years ago.'

Albert heard a car door slam, and moments later a key turned in the lock. He quickly put the phone down, and smiled.

# Stuck on You

## (from *And Thereby Hangs a Tale*)

Jeremy looked across the table at Arabella and still could not believe she had agreed to be his wife. He was the luckiest man in the world.

She was giving him the shy smile that had so bewitched him the first time they met, when a waiter appeared by his side. 'I'll have an espresso,' said Jeremy, 'and my fiancée' – it still sounded strange to him – 'will have a mint tea.'

'Very good, sir.'

Jeremy tried to stop himself looking around the room full of 'at home' people who knew exactly where they were and what was expected of them, whereas he had never visited The Ritz before. It became clear from the waves and blown kisses from customers who flitted in and out of the morning room that Arabella knew everyone, from the maître d' to several of 'the set', as she often referred to them. Jeremy sat back and tried to relax.

They'd first met at Ascot. Arabella was inside the royal enclosure looking out, while Jeremy was on the outside, looking in. That was how he'd assumed it would always be, until she gave him that beguiling smile as she strolled out of the enclosure and whispered as she passed him, 'Put your shirt on Trumpeter.' She then disappeared off in the direction of the private boxes.

Jeremy took her advice, and placed twenty pounds on Trumpeter – double his usual wager – before returning to the stands to see the horse romp home at 5–1. He hurried back to the royal enclosure to thank her, at the same time hoping she might give him another tip for the next race, but she was nowhere to be seen. He was disappointed, but still placed fifty pounds of his winnings on a horse the *Daily Express* tipster fancied. It turned out to be a nag that would be described in tomorrow's paper as an 'also-ran'.

Jeremy returned to the royal enclosure for a third time in the hope of seeing the lovely woman again. He searched the paddock full of smart men dressed in morning suits with little badges hanging from their lapels, all looking exactly like each other. They were accompanied by wives and girlfriends adorned in designer dresses and outrageous hats. Each one was trying desperately not to look like anyone else.

Then he spotted her, standing next to a tall, aristocratic-looking man who was bending down and listening intently to a jockey dressed in red-and-yellow hooped silks. She didn't appear to be interested in their conversation and began to look around. Her eyes settled on Jeremy and he received that same friendly smile once again. She whispered something to the tall man, then walked across the enclosure to join him at the railing.

'I hope you took my advice,' she said.

'Sure did,' said Jeremy. 'But how could you be so confident?'

'It's my father's horse.'

'Should I back your father's horse in the next race?'

'Certainly not. You should never bet on anything unless you're sure it's a certainty. I hope you won enough to take me to dinner tonight?'

If Jeremy didn't reply immediately, it was only because he couldn't believe he'd heard her correctly. He eventually stammered out, 'Where would you like to go?'

'The Ivy, eight o'clock. By the way, my name's Arabella Warwick.' Without another word she turned on her heel and went back to join her set.

Jeremy was surprised Arabella had given him a second look, let alone suggested they should dine together that evening. He expected that nothing would come of it, but as she'd already paid for dinner, he had nothing to lose.

Arabella arrived a few minutes after the appointed hour, and when she entered the restaurant, several pairs of male eyes followed her progress as she made her way to Jeremy's table. He had been told they were fully booked until he mentioned her name. Jeremy rose from his place long before she joined him. She took the seat opposite him as a waiter appeared by her side.

'The usual, madam?'

She nodded, but did not take her eyes off Jeremy.

By the time her Bellini had arrived, Jeremy had begun to relax a little. She listened intently to everything he had to say, laughed at his jokes, and even seemed to be interested in his work at the bank. Well, he had slightly exaggerated his position and the size of the deals he was working on.

After dinner, which was a little more expensive than he'd anticipated, he drove her back to her home in Pavilion Road, and was surprised when she invited him in for coffee, and even more surprised when they ended up in bed.

Jeremy had never slept with a woman on a first date before. He could only assume that it was what 'the set' did, and when he left the next morning, he certainly didn't expect to ever hear from her again. But she called that afternoon and invited him over for supper at her place. From that moment, they hardly spent a day apart during the next month.

What pleased Jeremy most was that Arabella didn't seem to mind that he couldn't afford to take her to her usual haunts, and appeared quite happy to share a Chinese or Indian meal when they went out for dinner, often insisting that they split the bill. But he didn't believe it could last, until one night she said, 'You do realise I'm in love with you, don't you, Jeremy?'

Jeremy had never shown his true feelings for Arabella. He'd assumed their relationship was nothing more than what her set would describe as a 'fling'. Not that she'd ever introduced him to anyone from her set. When he fell on one knee and proposed to her on the dance floor at Annabel's nightclub, he couldn't believe it when she said yes.

'I'll buy a ring tomorrow,' he said, trying

not to think about the awful state of his bank account, which had turned a deeper shade of red since he'd met Arabella.

'Why bother to buy one, when you can steal the best there is?' she said.

Jeremy burst out laughing, but it quickly became clear Arabella wasn't joking. That was the moment he should have walked away, but he realised that he couldn't if it meant losing her. He knew he wanted to spend the rest of his life with this beautiful and intoxicating woman, and if stealing a ring was what it took, it seemed a small price to pay.

'What type shall I steal?' he asked, still not altogether sure that she was serious.

'The expensive type,' she replied. 'In fact, I've already chosen the one I want.' She passed him a De Beers catalogue.

'Page forty-three,' she said. 'It's called the Kandice Diamond.'

'But have you worked out how I'm going to steal it?' asked Jeremy, studying a photograph of the faultless yellow diamond.

'Oh, that's the easy part, darling,' she said. 'All you'll have to do is follow my instructions.'

Jeremy didn't say a word until she'd finished outlining her plan.

That's how he had ended up in The Ritz that

morning, wearing his only tailored suit, a pair of Links cufflinks, a Cartier Tank watch and an old Etonian tie, all of which belonged to Arabella's father.

'I will have to return everything by tonight,' she said, 'otherwise Pa might miss them and start asking questions.'

'Of course,' said Jeremy, who was enjoying becoming accustomed to the trappings of the rich, even if it was only a fleeting acquaintance.

The waiter returned, carrying a silver tray. Neither of them spoke as he placed a cup of mint tea in front of Arabella and a pot of coffee on Jeremy's side of the table.

'Will there be anything else, sir?'

'No, thank you,' said Jeremy with an assurance he'd gained during the past month.

'Do you think you're ready?' asked Arabella, her knee brushing against the inside of his leg while she once again gave him the smile that had so captivated him at Ascot.

'I'm ready,' said Jeremy, trying to sound convincing.

'Good. I'll wait here until you return, darling.' That same smile. 'You know how much this means to me.'

Jeremy nodded, rose from his place and, without another word, walked out of the morning room, across the corridor, through the swing doors and out on to Piccadilly. He placed a stick of chewing gum in his mouth, hoping it would help him to relax. Normally Arabella would have disapproved, but on this occasion she had recommended it.

Jeremy stood nervously on the pavement and waited for a gap to appear in the traffic, then nipped across the road. He came to a halt outside De Beers, the largest diamond merchant in the world. This was his last chance to walk away. He knew he should take it, but just the thought of her made it impossible.

Jeremy rang the doorbell, which made him aware that his palms were sweating. Arabella had warned him that you couldn't just stroll into De Beers as if it was a supermarket. If they didn't like the look of you, they would not even open the door. That was why he had been measured for his first hand-tailored suit and bought a new silk shirt, and was wearing Arabella's father's watch, cufflinks and old Etonian tie. 'The tie will ensure that the door is opened immediately,' Arabella had told him, 'and once they spot the watch and the cufflinks, you'll be invited into the private salon, because by then they'll be convinced you're one of the rare people who can afford their wares.'

Arabella turned out to be correct, because when the doorman appeared, he took one look at Jeremy and immediately unlocked the door.

'Good morning, sir. How may I help you?'

'I was hoping to buy an engagement ring.'

'Of course, sir. Please step inside.'

Jeremy followed him down a long corridor, glancing at photographs on the walls that showed the history of the company since its foundation in 1888. Once they had reached the end of the corridor, the doorman melted away, to be replaced by a tall, middle-aged man wearing a well-cut dark suit, a white silk shirt and a black tie.

'Good morning, sir,' he said, giving a slight bow. 'My name is Crombie,' he added, before ushering Jeremy into his private lair. Jeremy walked into a small, well-lit room. In the centre was an oval table covered in a black velvet cloth, with comfortable-looking leather chairs on either side. The assistant waited until Jeremy had sat down before he took the seat opposite him.

'Would you care for some coffee, sir?' Crombie enquired helpfully.

'No, thank you,' said Jeremy, who had no desire to hold up proceedings any longer than necessary, for fear he might lose his nerve.

'And how may I help you today, sir?' Crombie asked, as if Jeremy were a regular customer.

'I've just become engaged . . .'

'Many congratulations, sir.'

'Thank you,' said Jeremy, beginning to feel a little more relaxed. 'I'm looking for a ring, something a bit special,' he added, still sticking to the script.

'You've certainly come to the right place, sir,' said Crombie, and pressed a button under the table.

The door opened immediately, and a man in an identical dark suit, white shirt and dark tie entered the room.

'The gentleman would like to see some engagement rings, Partridge.'

'Yes, of course, Mr Crombie,' replied the porter, and disappeared as quickly as he had arrived.

'Good weather for this time of year,' said Crombie as he waited for the porter to reappear.

'Not bad,' said Jeremy.

'No doubt you'll be going to Wimbledon, sir.'

'Yes, we've got tickets for the women's semi-finals,' said Jeremy, feeling rather pleased with himself, remembering that he'd strayed off script.

A moment later, the door opened and the porter reappeared carrying a large oak box which he placed dutifully in the centre of the table, before leaving without uttering a word.

Crombie waited until the door had closed before selecting a small key from a chain that hung from the waistband of his trousers, unlocking the box and opening the lid slowly to reveal three rows of assorted gems that took Jeremy's breath away. Definitely not the sort of thing he was used to seeing in the window of his local H. Samuel.

It was a few moments before he fully recovered, and then he remembered Arabella telling him he would be presented with a wide choice of stones so the salesman could estimate his price range without having to ask him directly.

Jeremy studied the box's contents intently, and after some thought selected a ring from the bottom row with three perfectly cut small emeralds set proud on a gold band.

'Quite beautiful,' said Jeremy as he studied the stones more carefully. 'What is the price of this ring?'

'One hundred and twenty-four thousand pounds, sir,' said Crombie, as if the amount was not worthy of note.

Jeremy placed the ring back in the box, and turned his attention to the row above. This time he selected a ring with a circle of sapphires on a white-gold band. He removed it from the box and pretended to study it more closely before asking the price.

'Two hundred and sixty-nine thousand pounds,' replied the same honeyed voice, accompanied by a smile that suggested the customer was heading in the right direction.

Jeremy replaced the ring and turned his attention to a large single diamond that lodged alone in the top row, leaving no doubt of its superiority. He removed it and, as with the others, studied it closely. 'And this magnificent stone,' he said, raising an eyebrow. 'Can you tell me a little about its origin?'

'I can indeed, sir,' said Crombie. 'It's a flawless, eighteen-point-four carat cushion-cut yellow diamond that was recently extracted from our mine in Rhodes. It has been certified by the Gemmological Institute of America as a Fancy Intense Yellow, and was cut from the original stone by one of our master craftsmen in Amsterdam. The stone has been set on a platinum band. I can assure sir that it is quite unique, and therefore worthy of a unique lady.'

Jeremy had a feeling that Mr Crombie might just have delivered that line before. 'No doubt there's a quite unique price to go with it.' He handed the ring to Crombie, who placed it back in the box.

'Eight hundred and fifty-four thousand pounds,' he said in a hushed voice.

'Do you have a loupe?' asked Jeremy. 'I'd like to study the stone more closely.' Arabella had taught him the word diamond merchants use when referring to a small magnifying glass, telling him that it would make him sound as if he regularly went to such places.

'Yes, of course, sir,' said Crombie, pulling open a drawer on his side of the table and extracting a small tortoiseshell loupe. When he looked back up, there was no sign of the Kandice Diamond, just a gaping space in the top row of the box.

'Do you still have the ring?' he asked, trying not to sound concerned.

'No,' said Jeremy. 'I handed it back to you a moment ago.'

Without another word, the assistant snapped the box closed and pressed the button below his side of the table. This time he did not indulge in any small talk while he waited. A moment later, two burly, flat-nosed men who looked as if they'd be more at home in a boxing ring than De Beers entered the room. One stayed by the door while the other stood a few inches behind Jeremy.

'Perhaps you'd be kind enough to return the ring?' said Crombie in a firm, flat, composed voice.

'I have never been so insulted,' said Jeremy, trying to sound insulted.

'I'm going to say this only once, sir. If you return the ring, we will not press charges, but if you do not—'

'And I'm going to say this only once,' said Jeremy, rising from his seat. 'The last time I saw the ring was when I handed it back to you.'

Jeremy turned to leave, but the man behind him placed a hand firmly on his shoulder and pushed him back down into the chair. Arabella had promised him there would be no rough stuff as long as he did exactly what they told him. Jeremy remained seated, not moving a muscle. Crombie rose from his place and said, 'Please follow me.'

One of the heavyweights opened the door and led Jeremy out of the room, while the other remained a pace behind him. At the end of the corridor they stopped outside a door marked 'Private'. The first guard opened the door and they entered another room which once again contained only one table, but this time it wasn't covered in a velvet cloth. Behind it sat a man who looked as if he'd been waiting for them.

He didn't invite Jeremy to sit, as there wasn't another chair in the room.

'My name is Granger,' the man said without expression. 'I've been the head of security at De Beers for the past fourteen years, and I used to be a detective inspector with the Metropolitan Police. I can tell you there's nothing I haven't seen, and no story I haven't heard before. So do not imagine even for one moment that you're going to get away with this, young man.'

How quickly the fawning *sir* had been replaced by the demeaning *young man*, thought Jeremy.

Granger paused to allow the full weight of his words to sink in. 'First, I must ask if you are willing to help me with my inquiries, or whether you would prefer us to call in the police, in which case you will be able to have a solicitor present.'

'I have nothing to hide,' said Jeremy haughtily, 'so naturally I'm happy to help.' Back on script.

'In that case,' said Granger, 'perhaps you'd be kind enough to take off your shoes, jacket and trousers.'

Jeremy kicked off his loafers, which Granger picked up and placed on the table. He then removed his jacket and handed it to Granger as if he was his valet. After taking off his trousers

47

he stood there, trying to look appalled at the treatment he was being subjected to.

Granger spent some considerable time pulling out every pocket of Jeremy's suit, then checking the lining and the seams. He failed to come up with anything other than a handkerchief. There was no wallet, no credit card, nothing that could identify the suspect, which made him even more suspicious. Granger placed the suit back on the table. 'Your tie?' he said, still sounding calm.

Jeremy undid the knot, pulled off the old Etonian tie and put it on the table. Granger ran the palm of his right hand across the blue stripes, but again, nothing. 'Your shirt.' Jeremy undid the buttons slowly, then handed his shirt over. He stood there shivering in just his pants and socks.

Granger checked the shirt, and for the first time the hint of a smile appeared on his lined face as he touched the collar. He pulled out two silver Tiffany collar stiffeners. Nice touch, Arabella, thought Jeremy as Granger placed them on the table, unable to mask how annoyed he was. He handed the shirt back to Jeremy, who replaced the collar stiffeners before putting his shirt and tie back on.

'Your underpants, please.'

Jeremy pulled down his pants and passed them across. Another check which he knew would reveal nothing. Granger handed them back and waited for him to pull them up before saying, 'And finally your socks.'

Jeremy pulled off his socks and laid them out on the table. Granger was now looking a little less sure of himself, but he still checked them carefully before turning his attention to Jeremy's loafers. He spent some time tapping, pushing and even trying to pull them apart. But there was nothing to be found.

To Jeremy's surprise, he once again asked him to remove his shirt and tie. When he had done so, Granger came around from behind the table and stood directly in front of him. He raised both his hands, and for a moment Jeremy thought the man was going to hit him. Instead, he pressed his fingers into Jeremy's scalp and ruffled his hair the way his father used to do when he was a child, but all he ended up with was greasy nails and a few stray hairs for his trouble.

'Raise your arms,' he barked. Jeremy held his arms high in the air, but Granger found nothing under his armpits. He then stood behind Jeremy. 'Raise one leg,' he ordered. Jeremy raised his right leg. There was nothing stuck under the heel, and nothing between the toes. 'The other leg,' said Granger but he ended up with the same result. He walked round to face him once again. 'Open your mouth.' Jeremy opened wide as if he was in the dentist's chair. Granger shone a pen-torch around his cavities, but didn't find so much as a gold tooth. He could not hide his worry as he asked Jeremy to accompany him to the room next door.

'May I put my clothes back on?'

'No, you may not,' came back the reply immediately.

Jeremy followed him into the next room, feeling worried about what torture they had in store for him. A man in a long white coat stood waiting next to what looked like a sun bed. 'Would you be kind enough to lie down so that I can take an X-ray?' he asked.

'Happily,' said Jeremy, and climbed on to the machine. Moments later there was a click and the two men studied the results on a screen. Jeremy knew it would reveal nothing.

Swallowing the Kandice Diamond had never been part of their plan.

'Thank you,' said the man in the white coat politely, and Granger added reluctantly, 'You can get dressed now.' Once Jeremy had his Etonian tie back on, he followed Granger back into the questioning room, where Crombie and the two guards were waiting for them.

'I'd like to leave now,' Jeremy said firmly.

Granger nodded, clearly unwilling to let him go, but he no longer had any excuse to hold him. Jeremy turned to face Crombie, looked him straight in the eye and said, 'You'll be hearing from my lawyer.' He thought he saw him grimace. Arabella's script had been perfect.

The two flat-nosed guards marched him off the premises, looking disappointed that he hadn't tried to escape. As Jeremy stepped back out on to the crowded Piccadilly pavement, he took a deep breath and waited for his heartbeat to return to something like normal before crossing the road. He then strolled confidently back into The Ritz and took his seat opposite Arabella.

'Your coffee's gone cold, darling,' she said, as if he'd just been to the loo. 'Perhaps you should order another.'

'Same again,' said Jeremy when the waiter appeared by his side.

'Any problems?' whispered Arabella once the waiter was out of earshot.

'No,' said Jeremy, suddenly feeling guilty, but at the same time excited. 'It all went to plan.'

'Good,' said Arabella. 'So now it's my turn.'

She rose from her seat and said, 'Better give me the watch and the cufflinks. I'll need to put them back in Daddy's room before we meet up this evening.'

Jeremy reluctantly unstrapped the watch, took out the cufflinks and handed them to Arabella. 'What about the tie?' he whispered.

'Better not take it off in The Ritz,' she said. She leaned over and kissed him gently on the lips. 'I'll come to your place around eight, and you can give it back to me then.' She gave him that smile one last time before walking out of the morning room.

A few moments later, Arabella was standing outside De Beers. The door was opened at once: the expensive necklace, the designer bag and the Chanel watch all suggested that this lady was not in the habit of being kept waiting.

'I want to look at some engagement rings,' she said shyly before stepping inside.

'Of course, madam,' said the doorman, and led her down the corridor.

During the next hour, Arabella carried out almost the same routine as Jeremy, and after much deliberate delay she told Mr Crombie, 'It's hopeless, quite hopeless. I'll have to bring Archie in. After all, he's the one who's going to foot the bill.'

'Of course, madam.'

'I'm joining him for lunch at Le Caprice,' she added, 'so we'll pop back this afternoon.'

'We'll look forward to seeing you both then,' said the sales associate as he closed the jewel box.

'Thank you, Mr Crombie,' said Arabella as she rose to leave. Arabella was escorted to the front door by the sales associate without any suggestion that she should take her clothes off. Once she was back on Piccadilly, she hailed a taxi and gave the driver an address in Lowndes Square. She checked her watch, sure that she would be back at the flat long before her father, who would never find out that his watch and cufflinks had been borrowed for a few hours, and who certainly wouldn't miss one of his old school ties.

As she sat in the back of the taxi, Arabella admired the perfect yellow diamond. Jeremy had carried out her instructions to the letter. She would of course have to explain to her friends why she'd broken off the engagement. Frankly, he just wasn't one of our set, never really fitted in.

But she had to admit she would quite miss him. She'd grown rather fond of Jeremy, and he was very keen between the sheets. And to think that all he'd get out of it was a pair of silver collar stiffeners and an old Etonian tie. Arabella hoped he still had enough money to cover the bill at The Ritz.

She dismissed Jeremy from her thoughts and turned her attention to the man she'd chosen to join her at Wimbledon. She had already lined him up to help her get a matching pair of earrings.

\*    \*    \*

When Mr Crombie left De Beers that night, he was still trying to work out how the man had managed it. After all, he'd had no more than a few seconds while his head was bowed.

'Goodnight, Doris,' he said as he passed a cleaner who was vacuuming in the corridor.

'Goodnight, sir,' said Doris, opening the door to the viewing room so she could continue to vacuum. This was where the customers selected the finest gems on earth, Mr Crombie had once told her, so it had to be spotless. She turned off the machine, removed the black velvet cloth from the table and began to polish the surface; first the top, then the rim. That's when she felt it.

Doris bent down to take a closer look. She

stared in disbelief at the large piece of chewing gum stuck under the rim of the table. She began to scrape it off, not stopping until there wasn't the slightest trace of it left. Doris then dropped it into the rubbish bag in her cleaning cart before placing the velvet cloth back on the table.

'Such a disgusting habit,' she muttered as she closed the viewing-room door and continued to vacuum the carpet in the corridor.

# Don't Drink the Water

## (from *Cat O' Nine Tales*)

'If you want to murder someone,' said Karl, 'don't do it in England.'

'Why not?' I asked innocently.

'The odds are against you getting away with it,' my fellow inmate warned me, as we walked round the exercise yard. 'You've got a much better chance in Russia.'

'I'll try to remember that,' I replied.

'Mind you,' added Karl, 'I knew a countryman of yours who did get away with murder, but at some cost.'

\*    \*    \*

It was Association, that welcome 45-minute break when you are released from your prison cell. You can either spend your time on the ground floor (which is about the size of a basketball court), sitting around chatting, playing table tennis or watching television, or you can go out into the fresh air and stroll around the edge of the yard (which is about the size of a football pitch). There was a twenty-foot-high concrete wall topped with razor wire, and only the sky to look up at – but this was, for me, the highlight of the day.

While I was confined in Belmarsh, a category A high-security prison in south-east London, I was locked in my cell for twenty-three hours a day (think about it). You are let out only to go to the canteen to pick up your lunch (five minutes), which you then eat in your cell. Five hours later you collect your supper (five more minutes). At that point they also hand you tomorrow's breakfast in a plastic bag, so that they don't have to let you out again before lunch the following day. The only other taste of freedom is Association, and even that can be cancelled if the prison is short-staffed (which happens about twice a week).

I always used the 45-minute escape to power-walk, for two reasons. One, I needed the exercise because on the outside I attend a local gym five days a week, and, two, not many prisoners bothered to try and keep up with me. Except Karl.

Karl was a Russian by birth who hailed from that beautiful city of St Petersburg. He was a contract killer who had just begun a 22-year sentence for disposing of a fellow countryman who was proving tiresome to one of the Mafia gangs back home. He cut his victims up into small pieces, and put what was left of them into a furnace. His fee – if you wanted someone disposed of – was five thousand pounds.

Karl was a bear of a man, six foot two and built like a weightlifter. He was covered in tattoos and never stopped talking. On balance, I didn't consider it wise to interrupt his flow. Like so many prisoners, Karl didn't talk about his own crime, and the golden rule (should you ever end up inside) is never ask what a prisoner is in for, unless they raise the subject. However, Karl did tell me a tale about an Englishman he'd come across in St Petersburg. He claimed to have seen what happened in the days when he'd been a driver for a government minister.

Although Karl and I were on different resident blocks, we met up regularly for Association. But it still took several walks around the yard before I squeezed the story of Richard Barnsley out of him.

*   *   *

DON'T DRINK THE WATER. Richard Barnsley stared at the little plastic card that had been placed on the basin in his bathroom. It was not the kind of warning you expect to find when you are staying in a five-star hotel. Unless, of course, you are in St Petersburg. By the side of the notice stood two bottles of Evian water.

When Richard (known as Dick) strolled back into his large bedroom, he found two more bottles had been placed on each side of the double bed, and another two on a table by the window. The management were not taking any chances.

Dick had flown into St Petersburg to close a deal with the Russians. His company had been chosen to build a pipeline that would stretch from the Urals to the Red Sea. It was a project that several other, more established, companies had wanted. Dick's firm had been awarded the contract, against great odds. But those odds had shortened once he promised Anatol Chenkov (the Minister for Energy and close personal friend of the President) two million dollars a year for the rest of his life. The only currencies the Russians trade in are dollars and death – especially when the money is going to be deposited in a numbered account.

Before Dick had started up his own company, Barnsley Construction, he had learnt his trade working in Nigeria, in Brazil and in Saudi Arabia for large corporations. Along the way he had picked up a trick or two about bribery. Most international companies treat bribery as just another form of tax, and make the provision for it whenever they present their offer to carry out work. The secret is always to know how much to offer the minister, and how little to dispose of among his workers.

Anatol Chenkov (who had been appointed by the Russian President, Putin) was a tough negotiator, but then under an earlier regime he had been a major in the KGB. However, when it came to setting up a bank account in Switzerland, the minister was clearly a beginner. Dick took full advantage of this as Chenkov had never travelled beyond the Russian border before he had been appointed to the Politburo.

Dick flew Chenkov to Geneva for the weekend, while he was on an official visit to London for trade talks. He opened a numbered account for him and deposited $100,000 – so-called 'seed money' – but more than Chenkov had ever been paid in his lifetime. This sweetener was to ensure that their bond would last for the necessary nine months until the contract was signed. It was a contract that would allow Dick to retire – on far more than two million a year.

*     *     *

Dick returned to the hotel that morning after his final meeting with the minister. He had seen him every day for the past week – sometimes publicly, more often privately. It was no different when Chenkov visited London. Neither man trusted the other, but then Dick never felt at ease with anyone who was willing to take a bribe because there was always someone else happy to offer him more. However, Dick felt more confident this time, as both of them seemed to have signed up for the same retirement policy.

Dick also helped to cement the relationship with a few added extras that Chenkov quickly became used to. A Rolls-Royce would always pick him up at Heathrow and drive him to The Savoy hotel. When Chenkov arrived, he would be shown to his usual riverside suite. Women then appeared every evening, as regularly as the morning papers. He preferred two of both – one broadsheet, one tabloid.

Now, back in St Petersburg, when Dick

checked out of the hotel, the minister's BMW was parked outside the front door waiting to take him to the airport. As he climbed into the back seat, he was surprised to find Chenkov waiting for him. They had parted after their morning meeting just an hour before.

'Is there a problem, Anatol?' he asked with concern.

'On the contrary,' said Chenkov. 'I have just had a call from the Kremlin which I didn't feel we should discuss over the phone, or even in my office. The President will be visiting St Petersburg on the sixteenth of May and has made it clear that he wishes to be present at the signing ceremony.'

'But that gives us less than three weeks to complete the contract,' said Dick.

'You told me at our meeting this morning,' Chenkov reminded him, 'that there were only a few *i*s to dot and *t*s to cross (an expression I'd not come across before), before you'd be able to finish the contract.'

The minister paused and lit his first cigar of the day, before adding, 'With that in mind, my dear friend, I look forward to seeing you back in St Petersburg in three weeks' time.' Chenkov's statement sounded casual. But, in truth, it had taken almost three years for the two men to reach this stage, and now it would only be another three weeks before the deal was finally sealed.

Dick didn't respond as he was already thinking about what needed to be done the moment his plane touched down at Heathrow.

'What's the first thing you will do after the deal has been signed?' asked Chenkov, breaking into his thoughts.

'Put in a bid for the water supply contract in this city, because whoever gets it would surely make an even larger fortune.'

The minister looked round sharply. 'Never raise that subject in public,' he said gravely. 'It's a very sensitive issue.'

Dick remained silent.

'And take my advice – don't drink the water. Last year we lost countless numbers of our citizens who got sick with . . .' the minister stopped, not wanting to add belief to a story that had been splashed across the front pages of every Western paper.

'How many is countless?' enquired Dick.

'None,' replied the minister. 'Or at least that's the official statistic released by the Ministry of Tourism,' he added, as the car came to a halt on a double red line outside the entrance of Pulkovo II airport. He leant forward. 'Karl, take

Mr Barnsley's bags to check-in, while I wait here.'

Dick leant across and shook hands with the minister for the second time that morning. 'Thank you, Anatol, for everything,' he said. 'See you in three weeks' time.'

'Long life and happiness, my friend,' said Chenkov as Dick stepped out of the car. Dick checked in at the departure desk an hour before boarding began for his flight to London.

'This is the last call for Flight 902 to London Heathrow,' a voice came crackling over the tannoy.

'Is there another flight going to London right now?' asked Dick.

'Yes,' replied the man behind the check-in desk. 'Flight 902 has been delayed, but they are just about to close the gate.'

'Can you get me on it?' asked Dick, as he slid a thousand-rouble note across the counter.

\*   \*   \*

Dick's plane touched down at Heathrow three and a half hours later. Once he had picked up his case from the carousel, he pushed his trolley through the 'Nothing to Declare' channel and emerged into the arrivals hall.

Stan, his driver, was already waiting among a group of chauffeurs. Most of them were holding up name cards. As soon as Stan spotted his boss, he walked quickly across and took his suitcase and overnight bag.

'Home or the office?' Stan asked Dick as they walked towards the short-stay car park.

Dick checked his watch – it was just after four. 'Home,' he said. 'I'll work in the back of the car.'

\* \* \*

Once Dick's Jaguar had come out of the car park to begin the journey home to Virginia Water, Dick immediately called his office.

'Richard Barnsley's office,' said a voice.

'Hi, Jill, it's me. I managed to catch an earlier flight, and I'm on my way home. Is there anything I should be worrying about?'

'No, everything is running smoothly this end,' Jill replied. 'We're all just waiting to find out how things went in St Petersburg.'

'Could not have gone better. The minister wants me back on May sixteenth to sign the contract.'

'But that's less than three weeks away.'

'Which means we will all have to get a move

on. So set up a board meeting for early next week, and then make an appointment for me to see Sam Cohen first thing tomorrow morning. I can't afford any slip-ups at this stage.'

'Can I come to St Petersburg with you?'

'Not this time, Jill, but once the contract has been signed, block out ten days in the diary. Then I'll take you somewhere a little warmer than St Petersburg.'

Dick sat silently in the back of the car, going over everything that needed to be covered before he returned to St Petersburg. By the time Stan drove through the wrought-iron gates and came to a halt outside the mansion, Dick knew what had to be done.

He jumped out of the car and ran into the house. He left Stan to unload the bags, and his housekeeper to unpack them. Dick was surprised not to find his wife standing on the top step, waiting to greet him, but then he remembered that he had caught an earlier flight, and Maureen would not be expecting him back for at least another couple of hours.

Dick ran upstairs to his bedroom, and quickly stripped off his clothes, dropping them in a pile on the floor. He went into the bathroom and turned on the shower, allowing the warm jets of water to slowly remove the grime of St Petersburg and Aeroflot.

After he had put on some casual clothes, Dick checked his appearance in the mirror. At fifty-three, his hair was turning grey early, and although he tried to hold his stomach in, he knew he ought to lose a few pounds, just a couple of notches on his belt – he would once the deal was signed and he had a little more time, he promised himself.

Dick left the bedroom and went down to the kitchen. He asked the cook to prepare him a salad, and then strolled into the drawing room, picked up *The Times,* and glanced at the headlines. A new leader of the Tory Party, a new leader of the Liberal Democrats, and now Gordon Brown had been elected leader of the Labour Party. None of the major political parties would be fighting the next election under the same leader.

Dick looked up when the phone began to ring. He walked across to his wife's writing desk and picked up the receiver, to hear Jill's voice on the other end of the line.

'The board meeting is fixed for next Thursday at ten o'clock, and I've also arranged for you to see Sam Cohen in his office at eight tomorrow morning,' Jill said over the phone. Dick removed a pen from an inside pocket of his blazer. 'I've emailed every member of the board to warn them that it's important,' she added.

'What time did you say my meeting was with Sam?'

'Eight o'clock at his office. He has to be in court by ten for another client.'

'Fine.' Dick opened his wife's drawer and grabbed the first piece of paper available. He wrote down, *Sam, office, 8, Thur board mtg, 10.*

'Well done, Jill,' he added. 'Better book me back into the Grand Palace Hotel, and email the minister to warn him what time I'll be arriving.'

'I already have,' Jill replied, 'and I've also booked you on a flight to St Petersburg on the Friday afternoon.'

'Well done. See you around ten tomorrow.' Dick put the phone down, and strolled through to his study with a large smile on his face. Everything was going to plan.

\* \* \*

When he reached his desk, Dick wrote the details of his appointments into his diary. He was just about to drop the piece of paper into a wastepaper basket when he decided just to check and see if it contained anything important.

He unfolded a letter, which he began to read. His smile turned to a frown long before he'd reached the final paragraph.

He started to read the letter, marked 'private and personal', a second time.

*Dear Mrs Barnsley,*

*This is to confirm your appointment at our office on Friday, 30 April, when we will continue our discussions on the matter you raised with me last Tuesday.*

*Remembering the full effects of your decision, I have asked my senior partner to join us on this occasion.*

*We both look forward to seeing you on the 30th.*

*Yours sincerely,*

*Andrew Symonds*

Dick immediately picked up the phone on his desk, and dialled Sam Cohen's number, hoping Sam hadn't already left for the day. When Sam pick up his private line, all Dick said was, 'Have you come across a lawyer called Andrew Symonds?'

'Only by reputation,' said Sam, 'but then I don't work on divorce law.'

'Divorce?' said Dick, as he heard a car coming up the gravel driveway. He glanced out of the window to see a Volkswagen swing round the circle and come to a halt outside the front door. Dick watched as his wife climbed out of her car. 'I'll see you at eight tomorrow, Sam, and the Russian contract won't be the only thing on the agenda.'

* * *

Dick's driver dropped him outside Sam Cohen's office in Lincoln's Inn Fields a few minutes before eight the following morning. The senior partner rose to greet his client as he entered the room. He gestured to a comfortable chair on the other side of the desk.

Dick had opened his briefcase even before he had sat down. He took out the letter and passed it across to Sam. The lawyer read it slowly before placing it on the desk in front of him.

'I've thought about the problem overnight,' said Sam, 'and I've also had a word with Anna Rentoul, our divorce partner. She confirmed that Symonds only handles marriage disputes, and with that in mind, I'm sorry to say that I will have to ask you some fairly personal questions.'

Dick nodded without comment.

'Have you ever talked about divorce with Maureen?'

'No,' said Dick firmly. 'We have had rows from time to time, but then what couples who have been together for over twenty years haven't?'

'No more than that?'

'She once threatened to leave me, but I thought that was all in the past.' Dick paused. 'I'm only surprised that she hasn't raised it with me before consulting a lawyer.'

'That's all too common,' said Sam. 'Over half the husbands who are served with a divorce petition say that they never saw it coming.'

'I certainly fall into that category,' admitted Dick. 'So what do I do next?'

'Not a lot you can do before she serves the papers, and I can't see that there is anything to be gained by raising the subject yourself. After all, nothing may come of it. But that doesn't mean we shouldn't prepare ourselves. Now, what grounds could she have for divorce?'

'None that I can think of.'

'Are you having an affair?'

'No. Well, yes, a fling with my secretary – but it's not going anywhere. She thinks it's serious, but I plan to replace her once the pipeline contract is signed.'

'So the deal is still on course?' said Sam.

'Yes, that's why I needed to see you so urgently in the first place,' replied Dick. 'I have to be back in St Petersburg for May the sixteenth, when both sides will be signing the contract.' He paused. 'And it's going to be witnessed by President Putin.'

'Congratulations,' said Sam. 'How much will that be worth to you?'

'Why do you ask?'

'I'm wondering if you're not the only person who's hoping that the deal will go through.'

'Around sixty million –' Dick hesitated – 'for the company.'

'And do you still own fifty-one per cent of the shares?'

'Yes, but I could always hide—'

'Don't even think about it,' said Sam. 'You won't be able to hide anything if Symonds is on the case. He will sniff out every last penny, like a pig hunting for truffles. And if the court were to discover that you tried to trick them, it would only make the judge feel more kind towards your wife.' The senior partner paused, looked straight at his client, and repeated, 'Don't even think about it.'

'So what should I do?'

'Nothing that will arouse suspicion; go about your business as usual, as if you have no idea what she's up to. Meanwhile, I'll fix a meeting with counsel, so at least we'll be better prepared than Mr Symonds will think. And one more thing,' said Sam, once again looking directly at his client, 'no more affairs until this problem has been sorted out. That's an order.'

\*     \*     \*

Dick kept a close eye on his wife during the next few days, but she gave no sign of there being anything wrong. If anything, she showed an unusual interest in how the trip to St Petersburg had gone, and over dinner on Thursday evening even asked if the board had come to a decision.

'They most certainly have,' Dick replied.

'Once Sam had taken the directors through each clause, gone over every detail, and answered all of their questions, they pretty much approved the contract.' Dick poured himself a second cup of coffee. He was taken by surprise by his wife's next question.

'Why don't I join you when you go to St Petersburg? We could fly out on the Friday,' she added, 'and spend the weekend visiting the Hermitage and the Summer Palace. We might even find enough time to see Catherine's amber collection – something I've always wanted to do.'

Dick didn't reply immediately, aware that this was not a casual suggestion as it had been years since his wife Maureen had accompanied him on a business trip. Dick's first reaction was to wonder what she was up to. 'Let me think about it,' he eventually said, leaving his coffee to go cold.

*     *     *

Dick rang Sam Cohen within minutes of arriving at his office and reported the conversation to his lawyer.

'Symonds must have advised her to witness the signing of the contract,' suggested Cohen.

'But why?'

'So that Maureen will be able to claim that over the years she has played a leading role in your business success, always being there to support you at those key moments in your career . . . '

'Balls,' said Dick, 'she's never taken any interest in how I make my money, only in how she can spend it.'

'. . . and therefore she must be entitled to fifty per cent of your assets.'

'But that could amount to over thirty million pounds,' Dick protested.

'Symonds has obviously done his homework.'

'Then I'll simply tell her that she can't come on the trip. It's not proper.'

'Which will allow Mr Symonds to change tack. He will then show you as a heartless man – a man who cut his own wife out of his life the moment he became a success, often travelling abroad, with a secretary who—'

'OK, OK, I get the picture. So letting her come to St Petersburg might well prove to be the lesser of two evils.'

'On the one hand . . . ' advised Sam.

'Bloody lawyers,' said Dick before he could finish the sentence.

'Funny how you only need us when you're in trouble,' Sam replied. 'So let's make sure that this time we anticipate her next move.'

'And what's that likely to be?'

'Once she's got you to St Petersburg, she will want to have sex.'

'We haven't had sex for years.'

'And not because I haven't wanted to, m'lord.'

'Oh, hell,' said Dick, 'I can't win.'

'You can as long as you don't follow Lady

Longford's advice. When asked if she had ever considered divorcing Lord Longford, she replied, "Divorce, never, murder, often."'

* * *

Mr and Mrs Richard Barnsley checked into the Grand Palace Hotel in St Petersburg a fortnight later. A porter placed their bags on a trolley, and then walked them to the Tolstoy Suite on the ninth floor.

'Must go to the loo before I burst,' said Dick as he rushed into the room ahead of his wife. While her husband disappeared into the bathroom, Maureen looked out of the window and admired the golden domes of St Nicholas's Cathedral.

Once he had locked the door, Dick removed the DON'T DRINK THE WATER sign that was perched on the washbasin and tucked it into the back pocket of his trousers. Next he unscrewed the tops of the two Evian bottles and poured the contents down the sink. He then refilled both bottles with tap water, before screwing the tops firmly back on and returning them to their place on the corner of the basin. He unlocked the door and strolled out of the bathroom.

Dick started to unpack his suitcase, but stopped the moment Maureen disappeared into the bathroom. First, he transferred the DON'T DRINK THE WATER sign from his back pocket into the side flap of his suitcase. He zipped up the flap, before checking around the room. There was a small bottle of Evian water on each side of the bed, and two large bottles on the table by the window.

Dick grabbed the bottle by his wife's side of the bed and retreated into the kitchenette at the far end of the room. He poured the contents down the sink, and refilled the bottle with tap water. He then returned it to Maureen's side of the bed. Next, he took the two large bottles from the table by the window and repeated the process.

By the time his wife had come out of the bathroom, Dick had almost finished unpacking. While Maureen continued to unpack her suitcase, Dick strolled across to his side of the bed and dialled a number he didn't need to look up. As he waited for the phone to be answered, he opened the bottle of Evian water on his side of the bed, and took a gulp.

'Hi, Anatol, it's Dick Barnsley. I thought I'd let you know that we've just checked in to the Grand Palace.'

'Welcome back to St Petersburg,' said a friendly voice. 'And is your wife with you on this occasion?'

'She most certainly is,' replied Dick, 'and very much looking forward to meeting you.'

'Me too,' said the minister, 'so make sure that you have a relaxed weekend because everything is set up for Monday morning. The President is due to fly in tomorrow night so he'll be present when the contract is signed.'

'Ten o'clock at the Winter Palace?'

'Ten o'clock,' repeated Anatol Chenkov. 'I'll pick you up from your hotel at nine. It's only a thirty-minute drive, but we can't afford to be late for this one.'

'I'll be waiting for you in the lobby,' said Dick. 'See you then.'

He put the phone down and turned to his wife. 'Why don't we go down to dinner, my darling? We've got a long day ahead of us tomorrow.' He adjusted his watch by three hours and added, 'So perhaps it would be wise to have an early night.'

Maureen placed a long silk nightdress on her side of the bed and smiled in agreement. As she turned to place her empty case in the wardrobe, Dick slipped an Evian bottle from the bedside table into his jacket pocket. He then accompanied his wife down to the dining room.

*   *   *

The head waiter led them to a quiet table in the corner and, once they were seated, offered his two guests menus. Maureen disappeared behind the large leather menu while she considered the table d'hôte, which allowed Dick enough time to remove the bottle of Evian from his pocket, undo the cap and fill his wife's glass.

Once they had both selected their meals, Maureen went over her proposed tour for the next two days. 'I think we should begin with the Hermitage, first thing in the morning,' she suggested, 'take a break for lunch, and then spend the rest of the afternoon at the Summer Palace.'

'What about the amber collection?' asked Dick, as he topped up her water glass. 'I thought that was a no-miss.'

'I have already booked in the amber collection and the Russian Museum for Sunday.'

'Sounds as if you have everything well organised,' said Dick, as a waiter placed a bowl of borscht – beetroot soup, a Russian favourite – in front of his wife.

Maureen spent the rest of the meal telling Dick about some of the treasures that they would see when they visited the Hermitage. By the time Dick had signed the bill, Maureen had drunk the bottle of water.

Dick slipped the empty bottle back in his pocket. Once they had returned to their room, he filled it with tap water and left it in the bathroom.

By the time Dick had undressed and climbed into bed, Maureen was still studying her guide-book.

'I feel exhausted,' Dick said. 'It must be the time change.' He turned his back on her, hoping she wouldn't work out that it was just after 8 p.m. in England.

*     *     *

Dick woke the following morning feeling very thirsty. He looked at the empty bottle of Evian on his side of the bed and remembered just in time. He climbed out of bed, walked across to the fridge and selected a bottle of orange juice.

'Will you be going to the gym this morning?' he asked a half-awake Maureen.

'Do I have time?'

'Sure, the Hermitage doesn't open until ten,

and one of the reasons I always stay here is because of the hotel's gym.'

'So what about you?'

'I still have to make some phone calls if everything is to be set up for Monday.'

Maureen slipped out of bed and disappeared into the bathroom, which allowed Dick enough time to top up her glass and replace the empty bottle of Evian on her side of the bed.

When Maureen emerged a few minutes later, she checked her watch before slipping on her gym kit. 'I should be back in about forty minutes,' she said, after tying up her trainers.

'Don't forget to take some water with you,' said Dick, handing her one of the bottles from the table by the window. 'They may not have one in the gym.'

'Thank you,' she said.

Dick wondered, from the expression on her face, if he was being just a little too considerate.

While Maureen was in the gym, Dick took a shower. When he walked back into the bedroom, he was pleased to see that the sun was shining. He put on a blazer and slacks, but only after he had checked that none of the bottles had been replaced by the hotel staff while he had been in the bathroom.

Dick ordered breakfast for both of them,

which arrived moments after Maureen returned from the gym, clutching the half-empty Evian bottle.

'How did your training go?' Dick asked.

'Not great,' Maureen replied. 'I felt a bit listless.'

'Probably just jetlag,' suggested Dick, as he took his place on the far side of the table. He poured his wife a glass of water, and himself another orange juice. Dick opened a copy of the *Herald Tribune*, which he began to read while he waited for his wife to dress. Hillary Clinton said she wouldn't be running for president, which only convinced Dick that she would, especially as she made the announcement standing by her husband's side.

\*  \*  \*

Maureen came out of the bathroom wearing a hotel dressing gown. She took the seat opposite her husband and sipped the water.

'Better take a bottle of Evian with us when we visit the Hermitage,' said Maureen. Dick looked up from behind his paper. 'The girl in the gym warned me not to drink the local water under any circumstances.'

'Oh yes, I should have warned you,' said

Dick, as Maureen took a bottle from the table by the window and put it in her bag. 'Can't be too careful.'

* * *

Dick and Maureen strolled through the front gates of the Hermitage a few minutes before ten, to find themselves at the back of a long queue. The crocodile of visitors moved slowly forward along an unshaded path. Maureen took several sips of water between turning the pages of the guidebook. It was ten forty before they reached the ticket booth.

Once inside, Maureen continued to study her guidebook. 'Whatever we do, we must be sure to see Michelangelo's *Crouching Boy*, Raphael's *Virgin*, and Leonardo's *Madonna Benois*.'

Dick smiled his agreement, but knew he would not be concerning himself with the masters.

As they climbed the wide marble staircase, they passed several magnificent statues. Dick was surprised to discover just how vast the Hermitage was. Despite visiting St Petersburg several times during the past three years, he had only ever seen the building from the outside.

Maureen read from the guidebook. 'Housed

on three floors, the collection displays treasures in over two hundred rooms. So let's get started.'

By eleven thirty they had only covered the Dutch and Italian schools on the first floor, by which time Maureen had finished the large bottle of Evian.

Dick volunteered to go and buy another bottle. He left his wife admiring Caravaggio's *The Lute Player*, while he slipped into the nearest rest room. He refilled the empty Evian bottle with tap water before rejoining his wife.

If Maureen had spent a little time studying one of the many drinks counters situated on each floor, she would have discovered that the Hermitage didn't stock Evian, because it had an exclusive contract with Volvic.

By twelve thirty they had all but covered the sixteen rooms devoted to the Renaissance artists, and agreed it was time for lunch. They left the building and strolled back into the midday sun. The two of them walked for a while along the bank of the Moika River, stopping only to take a photograph of a bride and groom posing on the Blue Bridge in front of the Mariinsky Palace.

'A local tradition,' said Maureen, turning another page of her guidebook.

After walking another block, they came

to a halt outside a small pizzeria. Its sensible square tables with neat red-and-white check tablecloths and smartly dressed waiters tempted them inside.

'I must go to the loo,' said Maureen. 'I'm feeling a little queasy. It must be the heat.' She added, 'Just order me a salad and a glass of water.'

Dick smiled, removed the Evian bottle from her bag and filled up the glass on her side of the table. When the waiter appeared, Dick ordered a salad for his wife, and ravioli plus a large Diet Coke for himself. He was desperate for something to drink.

Once she'd eaten her salad, Maureen perked up a little, and even began to tell Dick what they should look out for when they visited the Summer Palace.

On the long taxi ride through the north of the city, she continued to read extracts from her guidebook. 'Peter the Great built the Summer Palace after he had visited Versailles, and on returning to Russia employed the finest landscape gardeners and most gifted craftsmen in the land to copy the French masterpiece. He meant the finished work to be a tribute to the French, whom he greatly admired as the leaders of style in Europe.'

The taxi driver interrupted her flow with his own knowledge. 'We are just passing the recently built Winter Palace, which is where President Putin stays whenever he is in St Petersburg.' The driver paused.

'And, as the national flag is flying, he must be in town.'

'He's flown down from Moscow especially to see me,' said Dick.

The taxi driver laughed dutifully.

\* \* \*

The taxi drove through the gates of the Summer Palace half an hour later and the driver dropped his passengers off in a crowded car park. It was busy with sightseers and traders, who were standing behind their crude stalls plying their cheap souvenirs.

'Let's go and see the real thing,' suggested Maureen.

'I wait for you here,' said the taxi driver. 'No extra charge. How long?' he added.

'I should think we'd be a couple of hours,' said Dick. 'No more.'

'I wait for you here,' he repeated.

\* \* \*

The two of them strolled around the magnificent gardens, and Dick could see why it was described in the guidebooks as a 'can't afford to miss' attraction, with five stars.

Maureen continued to brief him between sips of water. 'The grounds surrounding the palace cover over a hundred acres, with more than twenty fountains, as well as eleven other residences.'

Although the sun was no longer burning down, the sky was still clear and Maureen continued to take regular gulps of water, but no matter how many times she offered the bottle to Dick, he always replied, 'No thanks.'

When they finally climbed the steps of the palace, they were greeted by another long queue, and Maureen admitted that she was feeling a little tired.

'Pity to have travelled this far,' said Dick, 'and not take a look inside.'

His wife agreed reluctantly.

When they reached the front of the queue, Dick purchased two entrance tickets and, for a small extra charge, selected an English-speaking guide to show them around.

'I don't feel too good,' said Maureen as they entered the Empress Catherine's bedroom. She clung onto the four poster bed.

'You must drink lots of water on such a hot day,' said the tour guide helpfully.

By the time they had reached Tsar Nicholas IV's study, Maureen warned her husband that she thought she was going to faint. Dick said sorry to their guide, put an arm around his wife's shoulder and assisted her out of the palace on an unsteady journey back to the car park. They found their taxi driver standing by his car waiting for them.

'We must return to the Grand Palace Hotel at once,' said Dick, as his wife fell into the back seat of the car like a drunk who has been thrown out of a pub on a Saturday night.

On the long drive back to St Petersburg, Maureen was violently sick in the back of the taxi, but the driver didn't comment, just kept a steady speed as he continued along the highway. Forty minutes later, he came to a halt outside the Grand Palace Hotel. Dick handed over a stack of notes and apologised.

'Hope madam better soon,' he said.

'Yes, let's hope so,' replied Dick.

Dick helped his wife out of the back of the car, and guided her quickly up the steps into the hotel lobby and towards the lifts, not wishing to draw attention to himself. He had her safely back in their suite moments later. Maureen immediately disappeared into the bathroom, and even with the door closed Dick could hear her retching. He searched around the room. In their absence, all the bottles of Evian had been replaced. He only bothered to empty the one by Maureen's bedside, which he refilled with tap water from the kitchenette.

Maureen finally emerged from the bathroom, and collapsed onto the bed. 'I feel awful,' she said.

'Perhaps you ought to take a couple of aspirin, and try to get some sleep?'

Maureen nodded weakly. 'Could you fetch them for me? They're in my wash bag.'

'Of course, my darling.' Once he'd found the pills, he filled a glass with tap water, before returning to his wife's side. She had taken off her dress, but not her slip.

Dick helped her to sit up and became aware for the first time that she was soaked in sweat. She swilled down the two aspirins with the glass of water Dick offered her. He lowered her gently down onto the pillow before drawing the curtains. He then strolled across to the bedroom door, opened it, and placed the *Do Not Disturb* sign on the door knob. The last thing he needed was for a concerned maid to come barging in and find his wife in her present state.

Once Dick was certain she was asleep, he went down to dinner.

'Will madam be joining you this evening?' asked the head waiter, once Dick was seated.

'No, sadly not,' replied Dick, 'she has a slight migraine. Too much sun I fear, but I'm sure she'll be fine by the morning.'

'Let's hope so, sir. What can I interest you in tonight?'

Dick took his time reading the menu, before he eventually said, 'I think I'll start with the foie gras, followed by a rump steak –' he paused – 'medium rare.'

'Excellent choice, sir.'

Dick poured himself a glass of water from the bottle on the table and quickly gulped it down, before filling his glass a second time. He didn't hurry his meal, and when he returned to his suite just after ten, he was delighted to find his wife was fast asleep.

He picked up her glass, took it to the bathroom and refilled it with tap water. He then put it back on her side of the bed. Dick took his time undressing, before finally slipping under the covers to settle down next to his wife. He turned off the bedside light and slept soundly.

* * *

When Dick woke the following morning, he found that he too was covered in sweat. The sheets were also soaked, and when he turned over to look at his wife all the colour had drained from her cheeks.

Dick eased himself out of bed, slipped into the bathroom and took a long shower. Once he had dried himself, he put on one of the hotel's towelling dressing gowns and returned to the bedroom. He crept over to his wife's side of the bed and once again refilled her empty glass with tap water. She had clearly woken during the night, but not disturbed him.

He drew the curtains before checking that the *Do Not Disturb* sign was still on the door. He returned to his wife's side of the bed, pulled up a chair and began to read the *Herald Tribune*. He had reached the sports pages by the time she woke. Her words were slurred. She managed, 'I feel awful.' A long pause followed before she added, 'Don't you think I ought to see a doctor?'

'He's already been to examine you, my dear,' said Dick. 'I called for him last night. Don't you remember? He told you that you'd caught a fever, and you'll just have to sweat it out.'

'Did he leave any pills?' asked Maureen.

'No, my darling. He just said you were not to eat anything, but to try and drink as much water as possible.' He held the glass up to her lips and she attempted to gulp down some more. She even managed, 'Thank you,' before collapsing back onto the pillow.

'Don't worry, my darling,' said Dick. 'You're going to be just fine, and I promise you I won't leave your side, even for a moment.' He leant over and kissed her on the forehead.

She fell asleep again.

The only time Dick left Maureen's side that day was to tell the housekeeper that his wife did not wish to have the sheets changed, to refill the glass of water on her bedside table, and late in the afternoon to take a call from the minister.

'The President flew in yesterday,' were Chenkov's opening words. 'He is staying at the Winter Palace, where I have just left him. He wanted me to let you know how much he is looking forward to meeting you and your wife.'

'How kind of him,' said Dick, 'but I have a problem.'

'A problem?' Chenkov was a man who didn't like problems, especially when the President was in town.

'It's just that Maureen seems to have caught a fever. We were out in the sun all day yesterday, and I'm not sure that she will have fully recovered in time to join us for the signing ceremony, so I may be on my own.'

'I'm sorry to hear that,' said Chenkov, 'and how are you?'

'Never felt better,' said Dick.

'That's good,' said Chenkov, sounding relieved. 'So I will pick you up at nine o'clock, as agreed. I do not want to keep the President waiting.'

'Neither do I, Anatol,' Dick told him. 'You will find me standing in the lobby long before nine.'

There was a knock on the door. Dick quickly put the phone down and rushed across to open it before anyone was given a chance to barge in. A maid was standing in the corridor next to a trolley laden with sheets, towels, bars of soap, shampoo bottles and cases of Evian water.

'You want the bed turned down, sir?' she asked, giving him a smile.

'No, thank you,' said Dick. 'My wife is not feeling well.' He pointed to the *Do Not Disturb* sign.

'More water, perhaps?' she suggested, holding up a large bottle of Evian.

'No,' he repeated firmly, and closed the door.

The only other call that evening came from the hotel manager. He asked politely if madam would like to see the hotel doctor.

'No, thank you,' said Dick. 'She just caught a little sun but she's on the mend, and I feel sure she will have fully recovered by the morning.'

'Just give me a call,' said the manager, 'should she change her mind. The doctor can be with you in minutes.'

'That's very considerate of you,' said Dick, 'but it won't be necessary,' he added before putting the phone down. He returned to his wife's side. Her skin was now pale and blotchy. He leant forward until he was almost touching her lips – she was still breathing.

He walked across to the fridge, opened it and took out all the unopened bottles of Evian water. He placed two of them in the bathroom, and one each side of the bed. His final action, before undressing, was to take the DON'T DRINK THE WATER sign out of his suitcase and replace it on the side of the washbasin.

\*     \*     \*

Chenkov's car pulled up outside the Grand Palace Hotel a few minutes before nine the following morning. Karl jumped out to open the back door for the minister.

Chenkov walked quickly up the steps and into the hotel, expecting to find Dick waiting for him in the lobby. He looked up and down the crowded corridor, but there was no sign of his business partner. He marched across to the reception desk and asked if Mr Barnsley had left a message for him.

'No, Minister,' replied the concierge. 'Would you like me to call his room?' The minister nodded briskly. They both waited for some time, before the concierge added, 'No one is answering the phone, Minister, so perhaps Mr Barnsley is on his way down.'

Chenkov nodded again, and began pacing up and down the lobby, continually glancing towards the elevator, before checking his watch. At ten past nine, the minister became even more anxious, as he had no desire to keep the President waiting. He returned to the reception desk.

'Try again,' he demanded.

The concierge immediately dialled Mr Barnsley's room number, but could only report that there was still no reply.

'Send for the manager,' barked the minister. The concierge nodded, picked up the phone once again, and dialled a single number. A few moments later, a tall, elegantly dressed man in a dark suit was standing by Chenkov's side.

'How may I assist you, Minister?' he asked.

'I need to go up to Mr Barnsley's room.'

'Of course, Minister, please follow me.'

When the three men arrived on the ninth floor, they quickly made their way to the Tolstoy Suite, where they found the *Do Not Disturb* sign hanging from the door knob. The minister banged loudly on the door, but there was no response.

'Open the door,' he demanded. The concierge obeyed without hesitation. The minister marched into the room, followed by the manager and the concierge. Chenkov came to an abrupt halt when he saw two still bodies lying in bed. The concierge didn't need to be told to call for a doctor.

\*     \*     \*

Sadly, the doctor had attended three such cases in the past month, but with a difference – they had all been locals. He studied his two patients for some time before he passed a judgement.

'The Siberian disease,' he confirmed, almost in a whisper. He paused and, looking up at the minister, added, 'The lady undoubtedly died during the night, whereas the gentleman has passed away within the last hour.'

The minister made no comment.

'My initial conclusion,' continued the doctor, 'is that she probably caught the disease from drinking too much of the local water –' he paused as he looked down at Dick's lifeless body – 'while her husband must have contracted the virus from his wife, probably during the night. Not an uncommon occurrence among married couples,' he added. 'Like so many of our countrymen, he clearly wasn't aware that –' he hesitated before saying the word in front of the minister – '*Siberius* is one of those rare diseases that is not only infectious but highly contagious.'

'But I called him last night,' protested the manager, 'and asked if he'd like to see a doctor, and he said it wasn't necessary, as his wife was on the mend and he was confident that she would be fully recovered by the morning.'

'How sad,' said the doctor, before adding, 'if only he'd said yes. It would have been too late to revive his wife, but I still might have saved him.'

| | |
|---|---|
| Amy's Diary | Maureen Lee |
| Beyond the Bounty | Tony Parsons |
| Bloody Valentine | James Patterson |
| Blackout | Emily Barr |
| Chickenfeed | Minette Walters |
| Cleanskin | Val McDermid |
| The Cleverness of Ladies | Alexander McCall Smith |
| Clouded Vision | Linwood Barclay |
| A Cool Head | Ian Rankin |
| A Cruel Fate | Lindsey Davis |
| The Dare | John Boyne |
| Doctor Who: Code of the Krillitanes | Justin Richards |
| Doctor Who: Made of Steel | Terrance Dicks |
| Doctor Who: Magic of the Angels | Jacqueline Rayner |
| Doctor Who: Revenge of the Judoon | Terrance Dicks |
| Doctor Who: The Silurian Gift | Mike Tucker |
| Doctor Who: The Sontaran Games | Jacqueline Rayner |
| A Dreadful Murder | Minette Walters |
| A Dream Come True | Maureen Lee |
| The Escape | Lynda La Plante |
| Follow Me | Sheila O'Flanagan |
| Four Warned | Jeffrey Archer |
| Full House | Maeve Binchy |
| Get the Life You Really Want | James Caan |
| The Grey Man | Andy McNab |
| Hello Mum | Bernardine Evaristo |
| Hidden | Barbara Taylor Bradford |

# Lose yourself
in a good
book with **Galaxy**®

*Curled up on the sofa,*
*Sunday morning in pyjamas,*
*just before bed,*
*in the bath or*
*on the way to work?*

**Wherever, whenever,**
**you can escape**
**with a good book!**

**So go on...**
*indulge yourself with*
*a good read and the*
**smooth taste of**
**Galaxy**® **chocolate.**

Proudly supports

## Other resources

## Enjoy this book?

Find out about all the others at **www.quickreads.org.uk**

For Quick Reads audio clips as well as videos
and ideas to help you enjoy reading visit the
BBC's Skillswise website **www.bbc.co.uk/quickreads**

Join the Reading Agency's Six Book Challenge at
**www.readingagency.org.uk/sixbookchallenge**

**THE**
**READING**
**AGENCY**

Find more books for new readers at
**www.newisland.ie**
**www.barringtonstoke.co.uk**

Barrington Stoke

Free courses to develop your skills are available in your
local area. To find out more phone 0800 100 900.

For more information on developing your skills
in Scotland visit **www.thebigplus.com**

Want to read more? Join your local library. You can borrow
books for free and take part in inspiring reading activities.

Quick Reads are brilliant short new books written by bestselling writers to help people discover the joys of reading for pleasure.

Find out more at **www.quickreads.org.uk**

@Quick_Reads    Quick-Reads

We would like to thank all our funders:

**LOTTERY FUNDED**

We would also like to thank all our partners in the Quick Reads project for their help and support: NIACE, unionlearn, National Book Tokens, The Reading Agency, National Literacy Trust, Welsh Books Council, The Big Plus Scotland, DELNI, NALA

At Quick Reads, World Book Day and World Book Night we want to encourage everyone in the UK and Ireland to read more and discover the joy of books.

World Book Day is on 6 March 2014
Find out more at **www.worldbookday.com**

World Book Night is on 23 April 2014
Find out more at **www.worldbooknight.org**